Dear Parents and Educators,

Welcome to Penguin Young Readers! ___
know that each child develops at his o___
speech, critical thinking, and, of course, reading. Penguin Young
Readers recognizes this fact. As a result, each Penguin Young Readers
book is assigned a traditional easy-to-read level (1–4) as well as a
Guided Reading Level (A–P). Both of these systems will help you choose
the right book for your child. Please refer to the back of each book
for specific leveling information. Penguin Young Readers features
esteemed authors and illustrators, stories about favorite characters,
fascinating nonfiction, and more!

Dinosaur Train™: Ride with Buddy

LEVEL **2**
GUIDED READING LEVEL **G**

This book is perfect for a **Progressing Reader** who:
- can figure out unknown words by using picture and context clues;
- can recognize beginning, middle, and ending sounds;
- can make and confirm predictions about what will happen in the text; and
- can distinguish between fiction and nonfiction.

Here are some **activities** you can do during and after reading this book:
- Character Traits: There are many different characters in this story. On a
  separate sheet of paper, write down the names of Buddy's friends with a
  list of facts about each of them. For example, Daphne has big feet.
- Sight Words: Sight words are frequently used words that readers must
  know just by looking at them. Knowing these words helps children
  develop into efficient readers. As you read the story, point out the sight
  words listed in the chart below.

am	find	of	she
eat	like	other	their

Remember, sharing the love of reading with a child is the best gift
you can give!

—Bonnie Bader, EdM
  Penguin Young Readers program

*Penguin Young Readers are leveled by independent reviewers applying the standards developed by Irene Fountas
and Gay Su Pinnell in *Matching Books to Readers: Using Leveled Books in Guided Reading*, Heinemann, 1999.

Penguin Young Readers
Published by the Penguin Group
Penguin Group (USA) Inc., 375 Hudson Street, New York, New York 10014, USA
Penguin Group (Canada), 90 Eglinton Avenue East, Suite 700,
Toronto, Ontario M4P 2Y3, Canada
(a division of Pearson Penguin Canada Inc.)
Penguin Books Ltd., 80 Strand, London WC2R 0RL, England
Penguin Group Ireland, 25 St. Stephen's Green, Dublin 2, Ireland
(a division of Penguin Books Ltd.)
Penguin Group (Australia), 250 Camberwell Road, Camberwell, Victoria 3124, Australia
(a division of Pearson Australia Group Pty. Ltd.)
Penguin Books India Pvt. Ltd., 11 Community Centre,
Panchsheel Park, New Delhi—110 017, India
Penguin Group (NZ), 67 Apollo Drive, Rosedale, Auckland 0632, New Zealand
(a division of Pearson New Zealand Ltd.)
Penguin Books (South Africa) (Pty.) Ltd., 24 Sturdee Avenue,
Rosebank, Johannesburg 2196, South Africa

Penguin Books Ltd., Registered Offices: 80 Strand, London WC2R 0RL, England

http://pbskids.org/dinosaurtrain

ISBN 978-0-448-45859-5   10 9 8 7 6 5 4 3 2 1

PENGUIN YOUNG READERS

LEVEL **2**

PROGRESSING READER

Ride with Buddy

Based on the television series
created by Craig Bartlett

Penguin Young Readers
An Imprint of Penguin Group (USA) Inc.

Hello.

My name is Buddy.

I am a T. rex.

Meet my family.

Tiny and Shiny are my sisters.

Don is my brother.

We have a mom and a dad.

We love to ride on the

Dinosaur Train.

Mr. Conductor takes us on trips
to meet other dinosaurs.

I like to visit my friend Annie.

She is a T. rex like me.

Annie and I have big

T. rex teeth.

We love being T. rexes.

This is my friend Tank.

Tank and his family have
horns on their heads.
They also have spikes
along their frills.

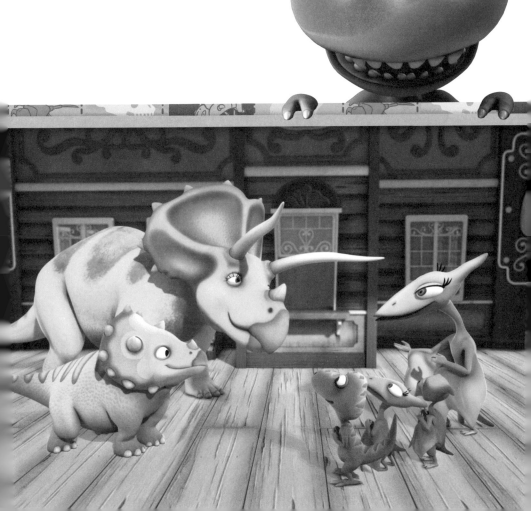

Tank has a baby brother.

His name is Tuck.

Tank and Tuck only eat plants.

Tank goes on many trips with my family on the Dinosaur Train.

This is our friend Lili.

Lili and Don go on trips to find rocks and shells.

At home, Don and Lili like to
find things, too.

We love having Lili and her family as our friends.

This is my friend Spikey.

Tiny and I like to explore

with Spikey.

Spikey and I look alike.

But Spikey has horns

on his head.

Spikey and I saw a lot of other dinosaurs with horns on one of our trips.

Meet Daphne.

She has big feet.

Daphne and her family taught us how to dance.

Stomp.

Stomp.

Look at Daphne dancing.

On our visit with Daphne,

our families stomped out

a dance together.

The Dinosaur Train takes us
across land and time.

We meet all kinds of dinosaurs.

The Dinosaur Train takes us
to all our friends: big, small,
spiky, or horned.